Wha

Beginners

Book One

Breach

By Jerome Vincent

The characters and events in this book are fictitious. Any similarity to real persons, living or deceased is coincidental and not intended by the author.

part of Williams Lea

Published by TSO (The Stationery Office), part of Williams Lea, and available from:

Online
www.tsoshop.co.uk

Mail, Telephone, Fax & E-mail
TSO
PO Box 29, Norwich, NR3 1GN
Telephone orders/General enquiries: 0333 202 5070
Fax orders: 0333 202 5080
E-mail: customer.services@tso.co.uk
Textphone 0333 202 5077

TSO@Blackwell and other Accredited Agents

Contact information

Full details of the range of material published under the ITIL® and RESILIA™ banners can be found at:
https://www.axelos.com/itil
https://www.axelos.com/resilia

For further information on qualifications and training accreditation, please visit:
https://www.axelos.com/resilia-qualifications
https://www.axelos.com/training-organization-benefits

For all other enquiries:
Email: Ask@AXELOS.com

ISBN 9780113314966

Contents

Foreword

Who Said Crime Doesn't Pay?

Ever had that experience that something is going very wrong but you're not quite sure why? That things are slipping out of control for no discernible reason?

The spread of networked computer systems across industry and business has made life a lot easier, a lot more efficient and a lot more creative. But innovation on this scale has inevitably brought some risk with it. And that risk has to be managed.

The only computer that is 100% safe is one that is switched off. But those who take their security seriously can drastically reduce the threats to their systems. This, in turn, means a decisive advantage over competitors.

Almost every week there's a news story about a big corporation that's been caught off-guard by hackers.

Often the direct financial damage of a security breach is minimal, but the reputational harm is immense. Household brands instantly become bywords for corporate carelessness. Seemingly impenetrable networks and systems are shown to be worthless, not because the technology doesn't work, but because the people who use them are careless.

In *Whaling for Beginners,* a short fictional account of one man's realization of his vulnerability and that of the company he worked so hard to build, we discover just how dangerous being a top executive can be. A simple mistake leads Jim Baines to fall victim to a carefully targeted cyber-attack. His company isn't resilient enough to withstand human error: his own. And, it turns out, nor is his biggest client, a giant food multinational that should really have known better.

This novella emphasises that leadership at the highest level is needed to protect organizations from 'whaling' attacks. Top executives are, quaintly, known as 'whales' in the hacking community and it's surprising how easy it is for hackers to stalk them. The novella also reveals that it's important to know your enemy: they aren't just after cash; they're after intellectual property and commercial secrets too. Most importantly, many of them just want to show the world how clever they are: a fact that makes them even more dangerous and very hard to combat.

Whaling for Beginners is not only a wake-up call for leading executives everywhere, it is a gripping and fascinating read in its own right.

Misha Glenny
Investigative journalist,
author and broadcaster

"I have been asked to teach a business class once I get settled in."

> Bernie Madoff in a letter to his daughter from Butner Prison, North Carolina, 2009 quoted in 'Swindle & Fraud' Lapham's Quarterly, Vol VIII, No.2 Spring 2015

Whaling: *Spear-phishing emails that target the upper management of all companies, corporations and public organizations, because of their unique access to sensitive corporate information and intellectual property secrets.*

Some hackers are looking to undermine the reputation of people and organizations they don't agree with or oppose because of their activities – for instance, relating to environmental or political concerns.

Whatever the motive – when the bosses get hacked everyone suffers!

Chapter

1

WildCat8 (Online)

WildCat8
Time to get the whale

NicholsonWay
Call me Ishmael

WildCat8
From *Moby Dick*? Predictably pretentious ☺

The piano groaned; violent chords clanging every time the old truck laboured around a tight curve. Ropes that looked like overused rubber-bands strained taut then slacked as the truck coughed out clouds of blue smoke. Jim feared for his life. It would be a strange twist of fate if he were to be crushed by an old, scuffed upright piano just like the one his mother used to play. The one she used to force him to practice his scales on when he was a child back in Dorset, England.

"But this is America!" Jim shouted. "You don't get crushed by old pianos in America!"

Jim kept his new car as far back from the truck as he could without grinding to a halt. A woman in a luxury SUV behind him was leaning on her horn. Jim threw her puzzled glances in his mirror – but she wasn't looking at him. She was screaming at a brood of kids eager for soccer practice, and the driver of the truck ahead.

The winding roads of Connecticut were beautiful at this time of year – mid-October in the lee of Halloween. The mid-morning sun was golden, and the reds, ambers, browns, and a million shades of ochre were enchanting. Jim loved to drive these roads. Usually they were empty. The odd old soldier out to get his paper, and a mail truck winding its way from mailbox to mailbox – but few others – just Jim and the glory of the fall.

Jim remembered the small street on which he grew up in a minor market town near the south coast of England. A limping postman with a bulging bag and a wry, experienced smile, stopping to chat with almost every householder whether they had post or not.

'Post!' Jim smiled. Americans called it 'mail' even if it came from the Post Office. When he'd come to America at the age of 25 – more than a quarter of a century ago now! Jim shook his head in disbelief – he'd asked how he could post a letter and got blank stares. He was a quick learner. Within a year he'd switched from British to American English but never lost his accent.

Jim braked suddenly. The piano looked as if it was about to tip forward onto the hood of his car, but it bounced back with a discordant clang.

The woman screamed and honked again.

A rugged arm appeared from the driver's side of the truck and waved apologetically. The guy was sure of his tethers and Jim decided that he had to trust him or just stop. He couldn't; he was already late for his meeting. And this meeting was a big one. He had an important presentation on his laptop, with copies on a specially branded Flash-drive. As CEO of Baines Packaging he had to be there. CEOs have to be where they have to be. A CEO's presence is what counts – sometimes more than his thoughts, plans or aspirations. Jim didn't mind. He'd worked hard to become CEO of the company and he wanted to make the most of his time at the top.

He didn't know that he was, in fact, a whale.

***

Crawford Sykes reached for the phone on his desk, hesitated, picked up the handset, then put it back down again. He sat back and rubbed his eyes, ran his bony fingers through his thin, grey hair, and pinched his craggy brow.

"Explain that to me again?"

"Turns out that ZanderTech outsource some of the

secondary printing work to a company in Laos," said the young woman sitting in front of Crawford's rough-hewn, pine desk. She was dressed in a mismatching array of what looked like thrift store clothes – her sweater looked as if it had been donated by a veteran of the Korean War (who'd worn it in combat!). Taryn Lowell. The newest and brightest member of Baines Packaging's IT team. She had a forensic mind, and a penchant for security. She distrusted every attachment or email until she was sure it was safe. Taryn was what marketeers call a Digital Native, though she hated the term. It just meant she'd grown up in the digital age when everything was – well, digital. Including crime. She wanted to be the Sherlock Holmes of cyberspace.

"Laos? Are you sure?" Crawford sounded indignant as well as surprised. He'd been to Laos – and Cambodia and Vietnam. A long time ago – and *not* for a vacation.

"Are you going to blink a lot and smack the side of your head and go postal?" Taryn said, smiling broadly. She liked to rile her boss.

"I hate all this outsourcing… offshoring… re-shoring… whatever they call it. Too complicated," Crawford growled.

"Why does anyone outsource anything for? It costs less. They make a better margin on what they sell to us. It's, like, *Global Capitalism*, Mr Sykes."

"Don't call me Mister."

"Sorry, Crawfie."

"Don't call me that either. Don't make me sorry that I hired you, Miss Taryn."

"It's Mzz – this is the third feminist era, dude."

"What?" Crawford got confused by Taryn's wry tone. As an IT guy who'd been around since even before the

CRAY Supercomputer in the 1980s, he understood valves, VDUs, chips and virtualisation… but not comedy.

"Be specific Ms Lowell. Tell me what got through from Laos," Crawford didn't want to indulge in idle chat anymore. He was worried.

"OK, it looks like we've been breached. So far…I know it's through ZanderTech and I think it was through their third-party supplier in Laos… but I'm not sure yet. All I know is that *someone somehow* has breached our defences. The hackers are lazily rummaging through all our data – right now. You need to tell Mr. Baines. Right now."

Taryn looked serious. Taryn hardly ever looked serious. She was a serious talent in the field of all things technical, but she was not a geek. She was nobody's cliché. She was Crawford might admit, if he was pressed, the future of the IT world. But she wasn't boring or narrow minded or even slightly anti-social. Some of his peers told him he had gone out on a limb when he'd hired her. She was the only woman on the IT team. But there was something about her tenacity and intuition to get things done and find things out. Right at that moment, Crawford didn't feel safe.

"My goodness, what do we do?" Crawford breathed heavily and rubbed his brow again, pinching the furrows so they turned from anxious red to a frightened white. This had never happened before. Crawford prided himself on running a tight ship in IT. He'd argued for strong defences. He'd made the case for substantial investment in firewalls and security training and fail-safe procedures to protect the company's proprietary designs and manufacturing methods. The assets and intellectual property that made Baines Packaging the success it was. That approach had helped win the company's contract with one of the nation's biggest food companies – SilasFoods.

"Jim's on his way to Silas now…"

"Call him. He has hands-free. Actually, he's the CEO – he should have a driver. Nice, burly one with a uniform." Taryn laughed, but Crawford didn't even register the joke.

"OK – I'll call him." Crawford picked up the phone and didn't put it down. He pressed auto-dial for Jim's cell phone. He sat and looked at Taryn as the call got routed, was hiring Taryn Lowell the best decision he had ever made?

***

Ercan sat back in the extra cheap copy of a very flexible ergonomic chair and felt as if he was going to fall flat on the wooden floor of the library. He grabbed the edge of the desk and pulled himself upright. Ever since they'd 'upgraded' the library, which sat in the shadow of Tottenham Hotspur Football Club's stadium in North London, he'd been unsure of himself. He'd been used to the dark, wood fittings that had survived since the 1920s. He hadn't minded the lack of light. He'd liked the smell of dust, the musty fragrance of old books retired to high shelves and never consulted save by old men with wild theories. He liked those old men. Some were cockneys and some were West Indian, many were old Turkish who all found common ground by being horrified by the changeable weather and constant grey cloud.

For Ercan, England was home. His country. He was Turkish only because his ancestry was Turkish. His parents had heavy accents, but they instilled in him a love of his new land: The land where he could thrive. And that's what he wanted to do; thrive. Only, he'd discovered that trying to do so in minimum wage jobs wasn't the answer. He'd had no love for school.

But Ercan excelled at maths. He had a brain that could solve equations in a heartbeat. His synapses had been lifted from a supercomputer – that's what his teacher at school said, when he was 15; when he was growing into a tall, good-looking, man with penetrating brown eyes, and a shock of black hair that would carelessly float above them. The girls loved him. The boys taunted him. He learned to fight. He knew he was better than them. Better than all of them. Smarter than anyone he knew.

But he was trapped. When he tried to get jobs – real jobs – in banks or big companies he was always rebuffed.

His accent was wrong. His background was wrong. His loping, casual style of walking and sitting and being were all wrong. He didn't fit in. Why should he play the game the establishment wanted him to play? Be the nerdy son of immigrants grateful for a chance to go to Oxford or Cambridge or Imperial College? Who would pay for that? Not his parents. Their grocery store was suffering. The big supermarkets had decided Tottenham was ripe for profit. The plum aubergines that used to fascinate Ercan as a kid now stayed in their boxes long enough to look forlorn and then – inevitably – appear on the family's dinner table too often.

He wanted to achieve more than that. He would not become a stereotypical man sitting in a greasy café or sport clubhouse, watching an obscure foreign soccer match on a big screen TV, drinking too much coffee and talking about the mother country.

Ercan would make money. Ercan would be the smartest guy online. Ercan would forge his own path.

And that's why he went whaling.

Not here. Not in this library. This was the clean place. Here he'd open up his legitimate laptop. It had his straight email accounts. He bought general items online on this computer. This was the computer that showed he was a legitimate citizen.

No, his real work was done in two internet cafes on Tottenham High Road. One near Seven Sisters underground station, and the other just past the bagel shop about a fifteen minute walk away from where Ercan was now.

He loved whaling.

Whaling was the best and biggest challenge for any hacker.

And he was good at it.

***

The truck wheezed to a stop at a light. The piano hummed. It was a surprisingly musical hum. A chord that made Jim smile. The phone rang. The dashboard display blinked – it was Crawford.

"Crawfish!" Jim shouted.

The woman in the luxury SUV screeched round Jim and squeezed into the lane next to the piano truck – as soon as the right turn light even thought about going green she gunned her engine and was off.

"Jim – are you alone?" Crawford sounded serious.

"No, I have four clowns in the car and we are off to the circus."

"Jim, be serious."

"Sorry, I should act like the CEO I am you mean? Will do. What's up?"

"How close are you to Silas?"

"Not as close as I should be. I took the scenic route. Big mistake. I love the fall and…"

"We have a problem."

"What kind of problem?"

"Security."

"Someone get in?"

"No… cyber security… I… listen… don't say anything at Silas… but… listen… the new Green Living range… the designs, the KPI's the… the everything… we think they've been breached…"

"You're not making sense, Craw, calm down. What do you mean 'breached'?" Jim said.

"Compromised. Security wise. Somehow… someone has got through our defences."

The truck pulled itself into the intersection and coughed out smoke again. Jim was glad to go slow. His brain was running through a thousand scenarios even though he couldn't make sense of what Crawford was telling him.

"Is this bad?" Jim asked. "Just tell me if this is bad."

"This is bad." Crawford's tone was funereal.

"Does it… I mean… is there an impact on Silas?"

"We don't know."

"We?"

"Taryn and I."

"Taryn?"

"Taryn Lowell."

"Oh… of course… does *she* understand what's

happened?" Jim liked Taryn. She was bright. He'd been to see her play in her latest band only last week – *Semblance Circus* – they'd covered a song by *The Cure* he really liked. Then one by *Joy Division* he liked even more. It took him back to the early 1980s – to the London he knew so well when he was at college. Back to when he'd met Hannah and Brandon. And now Brandon was half way round the world and Hannah was CFO at SilasFoods. Hannah trusted him and his company to deliver quality packaging for their global markets. A security breach could undermine all of that – in an instant. Just like he'd gone from thinking major Wall Street banks were made of solid granite to ones that might as well be made of balsa wood after repeated stories of them getting hacked…

"Are you listening to me?" Crawford said, sounding impatient now.

"I need facts… I need… time to think… but I can't cancel with Silas… if I cancel they'll suspect something."

"Just do the meeting as normal. If they say something… then… I don't know… stall."

"Stall? I can't stall. I'm the guy that's supposed to *know* what's going on!"

"So pretend to. You're good at that. It's how you got to where you are now."

Jim knew Crawford wasn't joking. From anyone else, a comment like that would be laced with friendly sarcasm. It would actually be an underhand compliment which celebrated one of Jim's great strengths – the ability to put people at ease by looking as if he was calm, knew what was happening, and could control events effortlessly – but Crawford never bought into that. He was uneasy unless he had concrete facts, and didn't like people who could bluff their way through a situation.

"Get me more details when you can." Jim ended the call. He was about to punch the horn in frustration when the truck carrying the battered piano turned off into what looked like a wrecking yard. Jim felt sorry for the piano. He also felt lost. He saw himself sitting at the keys of his mother's piano, staring at the yellow stained ivory. They reminded him of his grandfather's nicotine stained teeth.

"Keep going, son," Jim's grandfather always said, "Just keep going and soon, you'll be the only one left."

Jim always feared that something would appear that might undermine his achievements. But hackers? He never thought that they might be the cause of his demise.

"Come on! It can't be that bad!' he said to himself. He thought of the presentation on his laptop – the branded Flash-drives – the potential business he might lose. His company's reputation. *His* reputation. No – it would be OK. Crawford and Taryn would sort it out.

He drove on, a terrible feeling in his chest. He was not in control. Everything suddenly seemed beyond his control, and he did not like that feeling one bit.

***

Ercan stood at the checkout desk at Tottenham library. He'd found a short book about China. He was interested in China. He didn't quite know why. He was just interested. In front of him was a teenager arguing about a fine. She'd taken out a book to help her with a school project and then forgot it under her bed.

"I'm not paying. I never used it. My mum found it and... I never used it."

The librarian was calm and firm. He discounted the fine due to 'special circumstances' and avoided a confrontation. When Ercan give him the book about China the librarian smiled, "Interesting book," he said scanning it, "fascinating history."

Ercan nodded.

"You're always on your laptop... do you work in computers?" The librarian knew all his regulars and their quirks and interests.

"Something like that," Ercan said.

"You might be able to help us... on a voluntary basis... would you?"

"Sure... yeah... is there a problem?"

"We get all kinds of people using our computers," the librarian said turning to a row of basic PCs sitting along a wall at the far end of the library. Ercan had never used them. It was against his policy, internet cafes were where he did his business.

"You've got to be sure of your firewalls and filtering," Ercan said.

"Could you check it for me? I'd be very grateful. Save some poor kid from seeing something he or she shouldn't, or getting the whole lot infected with something awful." The librarian smiled broadly. His eyes were kind and fatherly. Ercan couldn't refuse.

"Sure."

"I don't understand all this technical computer stuff... but I know you've got to be careful of viruses and all kinds of bad computer code. Seems like you've got to be a boffin to understand it all." The librarian said handing the book to Ercan.

"It's people you have to worry about. People make the mistakes. People are always the weakest link," Ercan said.

The librarian frowned, he was curious. "You mean... for all the anti-virus subscriptions we have to pay it's the people who let the bad stuff in?"

"Always."

The librarian laughed. "Of course, 'twas ever thus. You'll read about it in that book. The Great Wall of China repelled invaders for... oh, two thousand years or so... and what made it finally fail? What caused it to be breached eventually? A man. It had been engineered to be secure – totally secure, but then in the seventeenth century a corrupt Chinese general accepted a bribe from the Manchu army – and they poured through to conquer China."

"Yeah, that's it. That's what happens now. Online." Ercan felt at home. He felt safe. The librarian made him feel like exploring whole new worlds.

***

WildCat8 (Online)

WildCat8
You're good – very good

NicholsonWay
Everyone tells me the same thing – it must
be true

WildCat8
Harpoon the big whale and it's bonus time

NicholsonWay
Harpoons loaded!

Chapter

2

WildCat8 (Online)

WildCat8
Those whales… they don't understand what's going on

NicholsonWay
That's why they're easy targets

WildCat8
Easy? Not so easy.

NicholsonWay
For me – easy.

"Is there a problem?" Hannah Simmons sat in the second chair to the left of where her CEO usually sat at board meetings. The boardroom was lined with walnut, Frank Lloyd Wright style, but was contemporary. It was a pastiche of an Art Deco era corporation. Jim had been in here many times, but today the décor struck him as false; corporate kitsch. A 1990s take on an era when real fortunes were forged in virgin markets. No one was spending this kind of money any more on boardrooms. Boardrooms had become dangerous places.

"A problem?" Jim clutched the polished arms of his plush chair.

"You look like there's something bothering you," Hannah could always see right through him. She had the first day they'd met at the London School of Economics. They'd both attended a lecture on Marxist economics and fled after a group of Trotskyites had started a fight. 1980 was a strange year: Thatcher, Reagan, The Cold War, Nuclear Oblivion. Jim felt nostalgic for the old certainties sometimes.

Suddenly he heard a song he remembered. A tinny version of 'Blue Monday' by New Order. A chill tumbled down his back and he shivered. It was Hannah's phone. She checked who the caller was and then refused the call.

"We're auditing a brand we're thinking of buying. It's bound to be bad news; or complicated news. Or news I don't need to hear. I'd rather talk to you." She smiled. Hannah was 55 but she looked 40. She'd worked hard all her life but looked as if she'd lived a life of leisure. Jim was sure that if she wrote a book about how she did it – it'd be a best seller.

"Something is wrong. You were distracted through your presentation. It was a *good* presentation, Jim, really good. I'll give it to everyone who counts." Hannah picked up one of the flash-drives Jim had given her. She smiled. "They can brand absolutely anything these days. We printed the face of our honey crunch doggie on smart phone cases for 10-year-olds. Do you know how many 10-year-olds have smart phones now? Amazing."

Jim chuckled unconvincingly.

"Are you having production problems? I hope not. We're already behind on launching Green Living in Europe and…"

"Everything's on schedule." Jim couldn't decide whether he should just come straight out and tell Hannah that there'd been a security breach back at Baines Packaging. He wanted to. But he didn't know the facts. He needed to know the facts. The damage. The extent of the breach. He decided to say nothing.

"Don't you love this time of year?" Hannah sat back and her chair smoothly swung round so she could look at the large windows that dominated one wall of the boardroom. A low cabinet hugged the wall beneath the window and ranged across its highly polished marble top were all the jewels of the SilasFoods family. They were some of the bestselling products on supermarket aisles and gondola-ends all over the world; products that generated billions in revenue. Some of which had made Jim very comfortably off indeed.

It could all be gone.

Jim couldn't shake the thought. But he had no idea of *what* was gone, or what the consequences of the hackers' intrusion might be, or even what they were after. If someone burgles your house it's usually clear what they want: money, jewellery, electronics... But a distant anonymous hacker was so much less tangible that he – or she – was somehow more intimidating. Jim realized that he'd never taken security seriously enough. It was something that – like your annually renewed anti-virus software subscription – just happened in the background while you got on with doing what you did best.

"Did you come all this way to be distracted?" Hannah was being playful, but very soon she'd start to be concerned. She'd get serious and start digging and he'd have to give in and spill the beans. He remembered his grandfather's exhortation again, 'Keep going! You can do it, lad.'

"I've always loved the fall. In England we only get an autumn. Nice but not spectacular." Jim smiled and sat up straight, and crossed his legs. He was back into his charming mode.

"How long have you been in America? Thirty years?"

"Twenty eight..."

"And you still act like you're English."

"I am English."

"Not even your passport is English... British... sorry... anymore."

"Always an Englishman – I'm Downton Abbey through and through."

"Yeah, sure... more like Downtown Manchester..."

"Your geography is appalling. I'm from Southampton. You even came to see my folks there once." Jim laughed.

Hannah nodded. "Strange days."

"Very strange."

They sat in silence for a moment.

"I'm going to go out and download every New Order album onto my phone and I'm going to relive every minute of our time at LSE on the way back," Jim said.

Hannah smiled – but it was a weak smile. Jim had judged the moment badly.

"You OK?" he asked.

She paused.

"Did you get a friend request from Brandon?"

***

Café Moussa was loud. An old hi-fi stack system sat on a sloping shelf above a counter where a coffee machine hissed and throbbed surrounded by displays of sugary treats. Moussa, the owner, chewed endlessly on some Somali delicacy. The old man's mouth was endlessly restless. He was either chewing or chewing and talking rapidly. He had three cell phones and one landline. He hardly ever used the landline. And if it did ring, it was the only time he turned the music down. A stack of old cassette tapes, labelled with an unintelligible scrawl, provided the music, which was East African, and sometimes North African, though Moussa had a soft spot for Italian chanteuse, Pietra Montecorvino, whose Neapolitan songs were spiced with Arab influences. Ercan hated her voice; it sounded like gravel from an air-purifier.

But the music and the chaos was what Ercan needed. Café Moussa was where he could do his spear-phishing and whaling. This is where he could hack with impunity. The rows of wheezing PCs were slow but safely anonymous. Ercan suspected that he wasn't the only hacker who used the place. He knew that, soon, he'd have to move on. There were many internet cafes in Tottenham. The area's population was constantly changing, but what did not change was the fact that most new arrivals could not afford a state-of-the art computer. So, they had to rely on places like Moussa's. That was lucrative for him and good for Ercan. IP addresses and internet connections were constantly shifting and morphing. It was hard for the authorities to track any one PC down.

Ercan adjusted his headphones. He liked it when he enabled the electronics to cut out the surrounding hub-bub. It tingled. He imagined he was in a force-field. He was separate from everything. His music helped him focus on his work. He was invincible.

The headphones were his only obvious ostentation. It didn't pay to spend money too freely. High-end designer clothes or electronics only attracted the wrong kind of attention. It paid to achieve the right balance – look as if you wanted to be rich, but make it obvious that you weren't. Because if anyone suspected you were, then they'd know that you were working on the dark side. And if they knew that then the cops would know it soon.

Ercan sat back and looked out through the streaky front window of Café Moussa. It was plastered with notices and advertisements scrawled on lined paper from school exercise books.

He turned to his screen and then felt a soft kiss on his cheek.

He turned. A young woman with large earrings that always reminded Ercan of the hoops lion tamers used at circuses was sitting in the seat next to him. Leila, his girlfriend.

"You doing what you do or you just hanging or what, like?" she said, exaggerating the local London accent.

Ercan pulled his headphones off and kissed her. "One day someone will clock you one," he said, "Talking like that."

"It's my manor and I'm gonna talk like I like, innit!" She laced her fingers through his and let her forehead rest on his shoulder. "Come home," she said in her normal voice.

"I'm working."

"This is work?"

"It's work. It's actual work. You know it is." Ercan scanned the café just in case any of the regulars had changed. He had to keep an eye on faces. New faces could spell danger. New faces could be cops.

"I worry, Ercan, I worry about you. About us. You could be…"

"Don't start." Ercan knew what she was going to say. She was going to try and talk him into applying for jobs again. Trying to get into a kind of corporation. He knew they wouldn't even look at him. And why should he work for someone else? They might have shiny new offices but they'd take too long to appreciate his skills. Ercan was an entrepreneur. He had ideas of his own. He was going to prove that he could make his own way.

"Let me get this done and we'll go home. Give me an hour. Promise."

Leila sat back, sighed, smiled, and stood up. Ercan couldn't help slow the scene down to admire her form. She was a beautiful girl. He was lucky. He stoked her forearm and pulled her hand to his lips and kissed her palm. "Love you."

She pouted, then assumed an exaggerated pose and

swaggered away. Behind the counter Moussa stopped talking into one or two phones – Ercan couldn't tell how many – and watched as Leila sashayed out onto the street.

Ercan felt proud. His life was good.

He turned back to his screen – the latest whale was in sight: Hannah Simmons, SilasFoods.

***

"We're working on something really special," Hannah said. She stood up and walked to the window. The view from the boardroom was spectacular: a vista of rolling wooded hills that looked like the palette of an artist. Splashes of yellow, red, orange, brown and green illuminated by the bright fall sun in a piercing blue sky. It was perfect. It reminded Jim, as it always did, of a painting by Frederic Church.

"Tell me, Jim, are you here?" Hannah was sitting on the edge of the board table right in front of him. He hadn't even noticed her move. He could smell her perfume; something floral, something expensive. Her body was still lithe and strong. He looked up at her.

"Sorry."

"Bad memories?"

"No. No not at all."

"When I saw Brandon's name on a friend request I froze," Hannah said.

"Did you accept?"

"Did you?"

"I did."

Hannah frowned. She crossed her arms. "Was that wise?"

"It's been a long time, Hannah and…"

"He's some kind of journalist now isn't he?" Hannah bit her bottom lip. She always did that when she was getting very serious.

"Whatever kind he is it's not the successful kind," Jim said.

"Sure but... he's... involved in all that anti-corporate stuff now isn't he?"

"He was but not anymore. He says he's doing a book about... something... I don't know. Brandon always talked big and never did anything substantial. But he's... harmless. I felt nostalgic. I can't say no... you know me... I feel guilty if I don't accept a friend request, It's insidious I know."

"People can see your world... all the people you know... I don't like it." Hannah crossed her arms and tensed up. Then she smiled and relaxed. "Let's not talk about Brandon." She leant closer to Jim, "I want to talk to you about next year's big project. This is a great opportunity for all of us. It's an entirely new recipe. Top secret!" she put her finger to her lips and winked.

Our competitors would kill for this particular recipe." Hannah pushed herself away from the table and walked back to the window. "And we're looking for an innovative packaging design. Really innovative. Think you can do it?"

"You know we can."

"Of course I do. Come on Jim... lighten up... times are good... we're on a roll here. I really think things are bouncing back. Let's put that nasty old recession behind us shall we?" She said the last line like a nurse treating a child with a high fever. Then she laughed. She turned back to the window.

"Don't you think of Frederic Church at this time of year? Don't you? I do. Remember when we all went to Olana down in New York and visited his studio and we all said we'd like to be nineteenth century bohemians... you'd be Church, with a big beard... and Brandon would be... the guy who took too many drugs... what was his name? Doesn't matter. And I'd be your muse." She laughed, then put her hands to her cheeks and stared out at the quilt of colours.

They sat in silence for a while. Then Hannah clapped her hands together as if she'd just had an inspiring thought. "Hey, why don't we take a trip down to the Hudson Valley River Museum. Talk business amongst the paintings... stare at the Palisades... watch the Hudson power its way to the ocean. How about it, Jim?"

Jim nodded. He wondered if, by the time they got to go, he and his company would be out of business. He felt sick. Everything he'd worked for – gone just because of some security issue. Some stupid mistake somewhere. He felt violated.

"You OK?" Hannah could see he was worried.

"I'm fine." Jim had never felt worse.

***

WildCat8 (Online)

WildCat8
Feels like the Cold War – only it's commercial

NicholsonWay
Cold War? I'll look it up ☺

WildCat8
You must be a baby

NicholsonWay
Yeah, Chucky from Child's Play!

Chapter

3

Crawford's office was as spare and as cold as an interrogation room over at the CIA's headquarters in Langley, Virginia. Jim had never been there, but he'd seen all the episodes of *Homeland* and Crawford's office reminded him of each intense scene. He sat across from Crawford looking at the small mirror over by the only bookcase in the room, a gunmetal affair bought from a local supplier who was on the verge of being a survivalist, and wondered if there were agents watching intently, recording his every twitch on video for later appraisal by a behavioural psychologist.

"I'll let Taryn explain it to you," Crawford said. He crossed his arms and Jim noticed that one of the pens he kept in the breast pocket of his polyester shirt was beginning to leak. He decided not to mention it. Crawford was an old friend, but not a good one. Jim had hired him to transform the production line and the design studio, and he'd done both brilliantly. But he'd slowed down. He'd lost his enthusiasm for technology. He was lagging behind in a fast-moving sector. Jim knew that he would have to do something significant to change that situation. But not now. Not yet.

"Where is she?" Jim asked.

"She'll be here. Don't worry." Crawford's knuckles were white. He was hugging his chest tightly, nervously. The security breach had clearly come as a shock to his system. His view of the world had changed. Jim could sense that he was out of kilter. He would have to tread carefully to keep Crawford stable. He needed to stay in control until this whole thing was cleared up.

"Are you OK?" Jim asked.

Crawford spun his chair round so he faced Jim. His

eyes were moist, and his jaw set firm. "I'm fine. Not fine because... because we've had this... this problem but..."

The door opened and saved him.

Taryn closed it quietly behind her. She held a tablet computer, a brand Jim didn't recognise. It was bright orange. A sticker for her band covered the manufacturer's logo. *Semblance Circus,* Jim wondered where the name came from.

Taryn pulled a steel chair up to Crawford's desk and placed it close to Jim's. She sat and pulled her long, floral skirt so it hung down over her legs. She wore red Converse sneakers with bright green laces. The laces had been added. Taryn could leave no fashion untouched: every item had to be individual – to her.

Jim tried to be as relaxed as he could. He slumped a little in his chair and let his chin rest on his palm, his elbow in the chair's armrest. He smiled at Taryn, "So, do we know what's happened and what's lost?" he said.

"What do think might have been lost?" Taryn asked.

"Umm, money, of course," Jim said.

"Money. Just money?" Taryn had adopted her Sherlock tone.

"Isn't that what they're after?" Jim knew that sounded naïve as soon as he'd said it.

"Hackers are hardly ever after just money." Taryn said.

"OK... credit-card numbers?"

"You don't take credit cards." Taryn smiled at Jim. She was enjoying baiting him. She knew he wouldn't mind. She could read him. He wasn't a scary CEO – he was a cuddly CEO, and she meant to always treat him that way.

"Yeah... good point. Then it must be money," Jim said,

and he looked at Crawford to see if his colleague could be of any help. Crawford shifted his gaze down to his well-ordered desk. He was not going to contribute to the conversation just yet.

"When was the last time you and the Board talked about security? And I don't mean the big guy in the uniform who strolls around looking beefy every day. I mean cyber security," Taryn said as if she already knew the answer.

Jim looked at Crawford, who was now staring up at the mottled ceiling.

"We… well, we discuss it…" Jim faltered.

"You discuss it, actively?" Taryn cut in.

"We've discussed it, yes… actively. In the past."

"How long ago did you last discuss it?" Taryn said.

Jim uncrossed his legs and sat up straight. Now he really did feel like he was in an episode of *Homeland.* He hoped it wouldn't tip over into *Twin Peaks* anytime soon. "Crawfie, you've got to help me out here… when we talk IT at board meetings we talk to *you*, after all!"

"We implemented a plan and the plan worked…" Crawford said, but he stopped. He was looking at Taryn. She had her head cocked as if they'd already had this conversation.

"…and the plan got really, like, amazingly old, correct?" she said.

Crawford looked at Jim as if to pass the buck; financial decisions were, after all, his ultimate responsibility.

"We invested in…" Jim began to say, but he couldn't recall the precise details of what IT security measures they'd spent money on.

"You invested in what exactly?" Taryn asked.

"In… look, we've never had a problem like this before and…" Jim was beginning to get annoyed. Not with Taryn. He was impressed with Taryn. Her tone was right. She knew the company was inadequately protected and she wanted to make the point the best way she knew how, by going right to the top – to Jim. But he was angry with himself. The horse had bolted and he was standing in an empty, compromised stable.

"You had problems before, didn't you?" Taryn said.

"Leonard Jones," Crawford said.

"Oh… Jones… he was one of our salesmen and he got a job over at Kappar Design and took a memory stick full of our proprietary stuff and… what's he got to do with it?" Jim said.

"He has nothing to do with this breach," Taryn said, "But I just want to make the point that when Jones took the software on that memory stick you called it theft even though he said it was his work and he owned it, right?" Taryn said.

"Yes, that's right but…"

"But you didn't protect your systems after that case… even though you successfully sued Jones and stopped him sharing the software with his new company."

"Didn't we? I don't remember." Jim was confused.

"We didn't." Crawford sounded sheepish. Jim looked at him and wanted to ask why but he didn't.

"Look… I've been on the road from Silas, Connecticut, and I'm tired and I nearly got crushed by a wild piano… and Hannah Simmons is counting on us to take packaging in new directions… and all the time instead of being really confident about the future of my company and everyone who works in it I have this gnawing feeling in my chest that something is terribly wrong and we're all on the verge of something really bad… and you're not telling me what the hell happened? Can you tell me what the hell happened in simple words so I can understand it, Taryn? Can you?" Jim sat forward and looked right into her green eyes.

"OK. You want to know the truth? The truth as I think it is right now?" Taryn looked at Jim with a steady, determined stare.

"Yes, tell me."

"The hackers got into your systems through your private email and they've not taken any money but they've copied the Green Living design files, and the breach wasn't some disgruntled employee who walked out with a memory stick… these hackers targeted a spear-phishing attack on you and they got what they wanted. But I don't think that's all they want. I think they're after bigger fish. In fact, they're on a whaling mission."

Jim stared at her. He didn't understand a word.

***

Leila uncoiled and stretched and yawned and let out a wail.

"Keep it down," Ercan said.

"What do you care? Robbie upstairs makes more noise than the whole of Tottenham put together and you don't say nothing to him!" Leila rubbed her eyes and then clicked her fingers into her right ear. "I'm going deaf," she said. Then she laughed. "I was too close to those speakers last night. Great gig though." She pulled her pillow around her head and covered her face. She let out a muffled yawn.

Then she let the pillow fall back and she said, "That better?"

Ercan smiled, kissed her and slipped out of the bed. He checked his phones. He had three.

Leila watched him. "I heard you last night…"

"Heard me what?"

"Talking."

"Yeah?"

"Talking to that… that American guy who sometimes calls…"

"What American guy?"

"Don't play games with me, Ercan, I'm not stupid." Leila sat up and reached for her packet of cigarettes. She thought better of it, and picked up a glass of water instead. She sipped it. She watched Ercan scroll through emails or texts or something on a PDA.

"I thought PDAs were, like, on the way out," she said.

"This one still works." Ercan smiled and put the phone down again.

"Is this guy, the Yank, Wildcat?"

Ercan frowned. He stepped back over to the bed and looked down at her. "Have you been snooping?"

"Yeah, so what you gonna do about it?" Leila playfully raised her fists like a boxer at the start of Round One.

"Don't."

"Who's the whale?"

Ercan sighed. He closed his eyes, thought for a second, and then looked back at Leila. "Moby Dick."

"Sounds like smut."

"It's a famous book."

"About a whale?"

"Yeah, about a whale – a big whale. The biggest."

"And, like, you're... after it too?"

"I might be."

Leila was enjoying the banter. She pulled her legs up her chest and rested her chin on them, "OK, so... the whale... is a person?"

"You ask too many questions."

"I was born inquisitive. I did some researching online..."

"That can be dangerous..."

"Hackers go whaling when they target these really important people... for whatever reason," Leila said, "And the reason is usually... I mean not usually... like... cash."

"OK."

"Apparently the Chinese and the Russians they do a lot of this stuff."

"Your research is pretty sound." Ercan began to make coffee.

"They're after secrets... and not just military secrets... military secrets are, like, so Cold War... what they really want is... ideas... business secrets... designs for cars and for machines and the latest, like, phones and stuff. That's big money. That's not taking pennies off a million transactions, that's big, big billions-style money."

Ercan turned to look at Leila. "You really have been doing your homework. Pity you never did it at school."

"Who needs school when I've got you."

"So, you think... that... I'm working for the Chinese or the Russians?"

"That would be too obvious."

"Yeah, much too obvious."

"Who's the Yank?"

"Just a link in the chain."

"And there is… like… some cash at the end of all this is there? A little? A smidge?" Leila wrinkled her nose.

"Yeah, a little."

"But you don't do it for the cash… of course."

"Cash is nice. But money isn't everything." Ercan poured the aromatic coffee and brought it back to the bed. Leila took hers and sat back, cradling the cup and letting the smell relax her.

"I wonder what it must be like to be that whale?" she said.

***

Jim was angry now. He balled his hands into fists and then relaxed them and then balled them again.

"My email address was the entry-point?" he said.

Taryn nodded, but then shook her head. Her hair fell over her eyes and she brushed it back. The bangles on her arms rung like meditation bells in a Buddhist temple. They calmed him slightly. He sat back and waited for her to explain.

"Turns out Laos has nothing to do with the first breach." Taryn said.

"Laos? I'd forgotten about Laos." Jim looked at Crawford who winced. He'd been on one of the very last tours of that war and the experience had scarred him. Not in the clichéd way most people assumed, but spiritually; he'd lost faith in humanity and turned to technology for comfort.

"I didn't even know we had anything to do with Laos," Jim said.

"Good point," Taryn said.

"Why is that a good point?" Jim asked.

"Because you assumed that cyber-security was all about technology when it's only partly about technology."

"Now you're talking in riddles," Jim said.

"You made a deal with ZanderTech in Germany to do… whatever it is they do…"

"Special laminates for juice cartons… it's revolutionary…"

"And cheap."

"Cost-effective, there's a difference."

Taryn smiled and nodded – the corporate speak was to be expected – then she said, "The reason ZanderTech's price for this revolutionary whatever-it-is is so low stems from the fact that they do business with a third party vendor in the Far East. It's the classic outsourcing chain… it extends right around the world. Globalisation red in tooth and claw."

"So?"

"So there are people involved at every stage and in every company and to be really secure you've got to know a lot about all the companies and people you deal with – ever – and you've got to make sure that they're as secure as they should be. You didn't do that. And nor did ZanderTech." Taryn shifted in her chair, "These chairs are really uncomfortable!"

Crawford ignored her. He was staring down at his desk. "She's right… ZanderTech are a sound company but… the new guy over there… Gert… he's been looking to increase his margins and he's outsourcing more and more work… and I don't think he did any checks."

"But… I still don't get what happened… how did this lead to me?" Jim looked at Crawford and then at Taryn and then back at Crawford, who gestured to Taryn to continue.

"The Far East connection could have been a source of the breach. My point is that neither you or ZanderTech did the checks you needed to do to make sure the whole supply chain was secure. The point is ZanderTech's flimsy security. They didn't have a robust password policy. Employees can use any old word from the dictionary if they want to. Any half-decent password cracking software can crack those kinds of passwords in a heartbeat. Or, huh, Heartbleed." Taryn chuckled at her topical reference. Jim and Crawford didn't get it.

"But how did the password cracking software get into ZanderTech?" Jim asked.

"There are a million ways – some sophisticated – some just plain stupid."

"And in this case?"

"Gert was lazy – and stupid. Someone did some research – through social or professional networking websites or just by searching the industry blogs – and they found that golf trip you went on to Hawaii in June."

Jim flinched. Golf trip? Yes, he went on an event run by one of the big manufacturing machinery suppliers in June. It was short but very boozy.

"OK… and?" Jim's heart beat faster. What else did she know about that trip?

"Lots of great pictures of CEO types grinning over their Nine-Irons or whatever it is those big sticks are called… and all their names and positions were plainly spelt out… and the relationships. Do you see?" Taryn wanted Jim and Crawford to follow the logic. She didn't want them getting lost.

"I see," Jim said.

"So, you and Gert are pals – which means you and Gert share both banter and pictures. The hacker does some spear phishing – he sends out emails to all the people who were at the event and offers to share great photos of holes-in-one and guys winning drinking competitions… that kind of thing."

"And someone bites." Jim could see the logic now. Simple but effective.

"And someone bites – namely Gert who got an email he thought was from you."

"Me!" Jim was stunned.

"It's easily done. If you don't check the email address or suspect that an email isn't quite right, because you're busy or… just careless… you click on it… see the attachment… download it and bang – malware swims through into your systems like a slippery electronic eel." Taryn was proud of her metaphor.

"Whales don't eat eels." Crawford said.

"Let's not worry about metaphors at this point, Crawford," Jim said. "Go on."

Taryn gathered her thoughts and continued. "Now Gert's laptop has the malware on it and the hacker knows it… and he can send out more whenever he wants so that as Gert opens applications and sends internal emails within his company, the infection spreads. That's when the password tool gets to work."

"But surely ZanderTech have anti-virus programs and all kinds of protection… just as we do," Jim said.

Taryn nodded, "Sure they do. But the hacker quickly creates what they call 'backdoors' – lots of them – so that as breaches are detected and dealt with others are still working. It doesn't take long to get what the hacker wants."

"And how does it get to us? Or is that an obvious question?" Jim said.

"It's an obvious question, but the right question," Taryn said, brushing hair that had slipped down over her eyes. "The hacker has quickly mapped out the VPN connections... including the fact that that's how you talk to your suppliers, mostly."

"Hold on... VPN?" Jim thought he knew what it meant but couldn't be sure.

"Virtual Private Networks – you don't communicate with your suppliers over the public internet – I mean, that would be stupid!" Taryn laughed.

Crawford looked at Jim and Jim looked at Crawford. They were thinking the same thing. Surely they did talk to some suppliers that way. That would have to change.

"So," Taryn continued, "The hacker can pretend to be an authorized user of the VPN between you and ZanderTech which means he can gain access to our systems and... do what he wants."

"Which is... go after SilasFoods?" Jim asked.

"Amongst other things. But, yes, go after them and, in particular, Hannah Simmons. The really big whale. Sorry, Jim. You're important, but... not like Hannah." Taryn smiled.

"OK... so our defences aren't good enough," Crawford said.

"No... no... the good news is... our defences are great! Even though you hardly ever talk about security amongst your very important board members... you have actually put in place some pretty good firewalls and anti-virus measures. But the hackers are cleverer than you are. They know there's always a weakest link."

"And that is?" Jim asked, knowing the answer.

"People. Like… you." Taryn said.

***

WildCat8 (Online)

WildCat8
Did the password work?

NicholsonWay
Didn't need it

WildCat8
What!? After my great detective work?

NicholsonWay
If it's too easy – it's just too easy

Chapter
4

Jim waited for Taryn to reveal – Sherlock Holmes style – the solution to the mystery; the legendary dog that didn't bark in the night time, or the simple mistake he'd made at some airport or on a social media website. Jim frowned: Hannah had been suspicious of Brandon Miles's friend request. Could he be the source of the breach? That was too far-fetched – surely?

"The hacker," Taryn continued, "had access to our Intranet before any of the malware was neutralised… and the hacker targets you, personally, and your personal email address, which he knows from looking at the information on the Intranet. OK? Does that make sense?"

"It makes sense," Jim said.

"Right, and then you make your simple mistake."

"I did? I mean, I do?"

"You do. You did. You wanted to get that presentation just right for your meeting with Hannah and so you emailed it to yourself… from your Baines account to your personal account and you worked on it at home… on your personal laptop… and then you transferred the final version onto a USB stick."

"That's exactly what I did." Jim actually felt relieved rather than embarrassed.

"Then you took it to Hannah and you gave it to Hannah… who gave it to… other important people."

"But don't SilasFoods have lots of security…?" Crawford said.

"They do but I don't think they have a policy preventing outside USB memory sticks from being attached to their computers. I checked – but they were vague about it." Taryn sat back. She'd made her case.

Jim looked at Crawford again. Both men sighed.

Then it occurred to Jim that the hacker would have had to know about his appointment with Hannah. He was about to ask, but then he stopped himself. Of course the hacker knew. He had access to his account for enough time to scan all his appointments.

Taryn stood up and said, "I'm late for a rehearsal, got to run."

She turned and left the room.

Jim suddenly felt like he was Brodie from *Homeland* – his first thought on entering the sparse room had spread through his body like a virus – a personal meme that put him on edge. He wasn't hiding anything. He wasn't the villain. He was the victim. His business was a victim. The situation felt like a domestic burglary. Was that a trite metaphor? Perhaps, but it's what it felt like. He felt violated – personally.

He jumped up and ran after Taryn.

"I'll take you to your rehearsal," he said.

She thought for a second and accepted.

"You don't mind me rushing out do you? I mean, work is great, but work is for daytime."

Jim admired her straight-talking. She didn't seem afraid of him. Jim was used to his executives being wary of his presence in meetings, or in their offices, or on the production floor. The tension came with the territory. He was their CEO after all. The position came with power, and power made people uneasy. You were the guy who could fire them on a whim. Jim had never fired anyone on a whim, but most of his people didn't know that. But, they did know that he was a fair man. He didn't enjoy his position in the company because it came with power. He put his responsibility to the people who worked for him and his shareholders first.

Which was why the security breach hurt so much. It hurt his pride. His sense of responsibility. His drive for excellence. The buck really did stop with him. Taryn's simple question had hit home: 'when was the last time you had a serious discussion with your board about cyber-security?'

He had to admit he'd taken it for granted. It was a technical issue. But it wasn't just that. It was a people issue too.

Semblance Circus played in a bar out on Route 202 and they had a gig on the weekend. The bar was closed on Monday nights and so they took the opportunity to rehearse their set.

"It feels like... like we've been... burgled. Does that make sense?" Jim said.

Taryn ignored him. "I love the smell of a new car. An expensive new car."

"This isn't that expensive."

"I thought CEO's had chauffeurs with cute little caps."

"Not in this company."

"Put it on the agenda of the next AGM, I'll vote for it."

"I like to drive myself."

Taryn began to run her finger across the buttons on the dash, "Oooo, passenger seat heating control... let's see... ahhh... nice."

They drove for a minute in silence as Taryn savoured the warming seat. Then she frowned. "Wrong time of year." She shut it off. "It's very like being burgled. You buy an expensive alarm and you think you won't get broken into… but all the alarm does is tell you you've been broken into really quickly… only the burglars, if they know what they're looking for, are out and away before anyone has time to react. Cyber-crime is even quicker than that. The big difference though, is that you don't usually give the key to the burglars long in advance… or tell them which flowerpot you hide it under. Stupid passwords or emailing sensitive documents using unsecure services… is… like… doing just that. So, sure, it feels like being burgled, only worse."

Jim nodded. He missed a traffic sign.

"Use your GPS… isn't that what it's for?" Taryn laughed.

"I know the way."

"Don't be so proud. You rely on technology for everything else."

She had a point. They stopped at a red light and Jim quickly tapped the name of the bar into the GPS – and it swiftly calculated a route. It was five minutes – the other way. Jim turned right on red and headed back the way they'd come.

"This is a secret…" Jim said. Then he stopped himself.

"Yeah?" Taryn sounded a little suspicious.

"I can trust you, right?"

"Sure you can. If I betray you, you can fire me," Taryn said.

"When I met with Hannah Simmons, at SilasFoods, she told me about a new recipe for a product… a new product they're going to launch worldwide… next year, I think."

Taryn waited for more – then when it was clear he wasn't going to add any detail, she said, "And this recipe is for?"

"Hannah didn't say."

Taryn looked puzzled, "Not much of a secret then is it."

"The point is… there is a new recipe. It's significant. Every new recipe is significant. That's why it's kept secret. The competition would pay a hell of a lot to get it." Jim thought his logic was impressive. "Could that be the point of hackers targeting us?"

Taryn thought for a second. She crossed her arms, and then uncrossed them. "Like I said, money is hardly ever the point when it comes to cyber-crime. Secrets are what sell for the really big bucks. Yeah, I guess, even though you don't know what this amazing new recipe is… I think you've got the motive. "

"So, Brandon Miles… maybe… maybe he is… a link in the chain perhaps?"

"The guy you went to college with?"

"Hannah and I did, yes, in London… The London School of Economics…"

"Cool school!"

"Could his sudden reappearance… I mean… could that be… a clue?"

"Too obvious. Hackers are cleverer than that. But, you never know. Where is this guy?"

"I don't know. He's just… on a social media website."

"Ah, the other country… the shadow world… Here!"

Taryn pointed at the bar. Jim swerved into its parking-lot. A trucker behind him raged and pulled on his siren sized horn. Jim pulled up at the entrance. *Ludwig's Rest* – Jim had met the Bavarian owner, a grizzly German with an enormous appetite for lager.

Taryn stayed in her seat, her hands on her lap. She was thinking. Then she said,

"You're a whale and Hannah Simmons is a bigger whale. Brandon knows that. He's not the hacker. He wouldn't contact you if he was the hacker. Hackers are intelligent people. I mean – really smart people. There might be like... just a couple of hundred good ones in the entire world! Which is why, if you ask me, and some Harvard Law School type suits, they should be tracked down and..."

"Put in jail?"

"Given nice, high-paid jobs in the CIA and the FBI: Then you'd end cyber-crime in a heartbeat."

Taryn laughed, opened the door and jumped out. She pulled her guitar case from the back seat and leaned back into the car, "Thanks for the lift. Want to stay and hear the set?"

Jim looked at his watch. He had work to do. But, perhaps, he also needed time to think. And listening to music might help.

"Sure," he said.

***

"Ever wondered about why there are so many bugs?" Ercan said.

Leila was trying to spear a maraschino cherry in her cocktail. It had slipped from the plastic sword on which it had been impaled by the bartender. They were sitting in *Charlie's* – a new bar on the intersection between Lordship Lane and White Hart Lane.

"Bug? Like, you mean, insects?

"No, in software. Coding software is hard. That's why there are so many bugs. Some are like grammatical mistakes. Some are copying errors. Like, in ancient times when a monk was asked to copy a book – you know... an illuminated manuscript... before there was, like, printing..."

"What are you on?" Leila liked to listen despite her sarcasm.

"...and he'd make a little mistake – write one word when he meant to write another and then that word gets copied into the next version and suddenly the meaning is different and before you know it there's a religious war on!" Ercan smiled. He was proud of his metaphor. Leila downed her drink and sighed.

"Every piece of software out there has a bug in it. Some has a bug every four or five lines of code! That's my raw material. That's my food and drink," Ercan said.

"Bugs are protein for geeks!" Leila laughed.

"There could be a bug deep in the software... almost down to the machine code... that's just been sitting there for years... 25 years! Like Shellshock. That was a really old bug... it took them a lifetime to find... and only the best of our kind search them out and... bang! We're in."

Leila pushed the cocktail glass away.

"You're full of yourself tonight."

"Yeah, I am. I got the whale."

***

WildCat8 (Online)

WildCat8
We need this whale beached

NicholsonWay
Sure – immobilize – then strip it down – will do

WildCat8
Down to the real secrets – top dollar secrets

NicholsonWay
Secrets don't exist anymore – be in touch

Hannah Simmons froze when Patrick LeBlanc, SilasFoods' CIO, unfolded a large A3 spreadsheet over the files on her desk and got to the point; the bottom line – the price. That was what Hannah was interested in. Usually.

But this evening the bottom-line was not a string of numbers but a problem – a danger – a breach in security.

"Somehow malware was introduced into our systems. And I am not talking about some low-level employee clicking on something in an email or on a porn site; I'm talking about a malicious program directly introduced in the last day or so by someone... someone..."

Patrick was going over the phrase he'd obviously prepared before knocking on her office door. Hannah rapidly thought through her meetings and movements over the last week or so. She hadn't done anything. She'd hardly been online. She'd answered internal and external emails, but had spent most of her week writing a report by hand, with a pen on a legal pad.

"I don't understand, Patrick, or at least, I don't think I do. Are you telling me that I had something to do with this... this security breach? How bad is it anyway?" Hannah didn't like Patrick. She thought him pretentious and sexist. He was young, for a C-level executive, but old-school. She suspected he'd had a lot to do with the appointment of the new CEO – a Canadian compatriot. A man intent on change to build his reputation.

"You had a meeting with Mr. Baines. From Baines Packaging. Your old friend. Yes?" Patrick folded the spreadsheet. It was clear he didn't think it worth going through the fine detail of the technical aspects of the breach. Hannah's combative mood precluded it.

"I did. But…" Hannah froze again. This time she could feel the ice crystals form across her back and her legs and her arms – she could see Jim hand over the USB memory stick.

"He gave you a flash-drive?"

"A memory-stick."

"Same thing."

"Yes, he gave me a flash-drive. It had his presentation on it. He always gives us a flash-drive." Hannah tried to think if there was something she should have done; some policy that had been detailed in a memo she hadn't read. But then she remembered a memo she'd written a year ago. She shivered.

"We have a policy not to introduce flash-drives into our system which come from third-parties." Patrick folded his arms. He was preparing to accuse her, but he was hoping she'd just admit to her mistake.

"We do?"

"Hannah, you *know* we do."

"OK, so we have a policy but…"

"But you exempted yourself from it," Patrick interjected. "It is standard procedure in organizations like ours."

"I always used approved memory-sticks…" Hannah suddenly felt like a school-girl in a Principal's office.

"On June 18 last year…"

Hannah closed her eyes. She remembered writing the memo. She'd been stuck at a conference in Argentina and wanted to update a presentation with material from an economics professor who'd been asked to appear with her at a Q&A session. She'd asked for exemption from the 'No-Outside-USB' policy to get his research numbers downloaded into her PowerPoint. Her fellow directors had agreed. Nothing bad happened. They'd all just continued flouting the security policy believing that they, the members of the Board, were immune from attack. It was stupid, but it hadn't felt stupid till now – this moment – with Patrick staring at her as if she were an errant teen.

"If we'd been challenged – at the time – really challenged, then... then we would have gone back to adhering to the policy..." Hannah knew she couldn't argue her way out of the problem. "We're just people, you know, and people make mistakes."

Patrick ignored her plea. She knew it must have sounded pathetic.

"Mr. Baines gave you the memory-stick which contained malware. This has infected our systems. The new recipe has been compromised."

Hannah slammed her fist on the desk. Patrick jumped. He'd never seen her this angry before. "Are you accusing Jim?"

"No... it was... most probably unwitting... on his part"

"Unwitting? On his part?"

"His company has been breached too... I just got off the phone with Crawford Sykes... their IT head and he..."

"But Jim didn't know that when he was here, surely."

"No. He didn't. That is what Mr. Sykes told me." Patrick stared at Hannah for a moment. He suspected there was more to her relationship with Jim – something deep and distant in time – but he could never ask her about it. He knew she wouldn't tell him.

"Have we lost money? Have they compromised our accounts... our customer records... what have they done?" Hannah didn't want to accept that the new recipe had been stolen. She knew, in her heart, that the new recipe and all the culinary and production secrets behind their best-selling brands would be a big prize for... for whom?

"They were not after money, just our IP. IP is worth more. It is after all 'property' – intellectual property is where the big money is because mere cash just gets spent, but ideas can be turned into cash for many, many years." Patrick uncrossed his arms and put his hands on his knees. He could see how much the news had hurt Hannah. He lost the will to try and best her with either argument or guilt.

"What do we do?" Hannah asked.

"We have cut links with Baines for now – and we're reviewing our systems." Patrick hesitated and then said, with more sympathy in his voice, "Hannah, this is not your fault. Directly."

"Not my fault... directly? But it's my fault... indirectly?"

Patrick stood up and gathered his papers. He looked down at Hannah and she could tell that he now felt sorry for her. She knew she was lost.

"In the end, we had a definite policy about memory sticks or flash drives, whatever you want to call them, but we were all lax in allowing certain members of the team... the Board in particular... to get round it. That encouraged some of us to take work home on them and then bring them back after connecting them with our home computers or even public computers. We were lucky for a long time. Nothing happened. But now, with this breach, we have experienced a very targeted attack. Someone targeted you: you specifically. They used Jim as the mule. An unwitting mule. They identified him and understood his connections... to you. They took a chance on him and it paid off. He was a whale and you were the bigger whale."

Hannah frowned, "Whale?"

"Yes, important, high-value targets. Someone knows a lot about you. And that someone is mixed up in very bad things."

Patrick left the room.

Hannah knew she would not be fired. That would be unseemly. It would only bring attention to SilasFoods and its security failings. She began to compose her resignation in her head.

***

Listening to Taryn's band, *Semblance Circus,* proved to be unsettling for Jim. He sat at the back of the empty bar, its owner carelessly wiping glasses and eyeing Jim suspiciously, and waited for the three young guys and Taryn to tune up and sort out their electronics. Jim reached for a napkin and found a pen in his jacket and began to draw a simple diagram. Baines Packaging was linked to ZanderTech which was linked to whatever the Laos company was called. That was one point of vulnerability.

Then Jim drew a little stick-figure and wrote 'Gert' over its head. Then he drew a line to Baines Packaging and put another stick-figure standing on its box. He wrote 'Jim' on it. Then he crossed out 'Jim' and wrote 'me.'

At the top of the page he put another two or three stick-figures and wrote 'hackers' – then thought for a moment and added, 'Brandon?' – more lines radiated out to both ZanderTech, the Far Eastern company, and Baines. Jim drew a big box at the bottom of the page – 'Silas' – he added his last stick-figure, 'Hannah' – then he drew a whale with wavy water lines around it and a harpoon aimed at its heart.

He put a cross through 'me' and wrote 'careless' then scrunched up the paper.

Jim's arrows and boxes had looked like Mondrian after too many Anisettes, but he liked the flow he'd visualized. It made sense to him now. It also brought into sharp focus just how small and dangerous a world digital technology was creating. It probably took just a few seconds for the criminals to open up pathways that they could exploit for profit – or just plain malice. Hackers weren't all criminals, some were campaigners; others were terrorists.

When the band began to play Jim's frontal cortex froze. A vivid memory formed within the first three notes of the first song. He found himself short of breath. *Semblance Circus* were playing 'Move Closer' – an eighties hit that Jim hadn't heard in years.

It had been on the radio the morning he awoke next to Hannah back in 1985 in her small flat off Tavistock Square, close to the London School of Economics. It was a cool but bright November morning, and the street below was busy with commuter traffic and three magpies were pecking at something on the bedroom windowsill. The image and the sounds were as vivid and exciting as they had been thirty years before. Jim could see Hannah lying like Cleopatra wrapped in a golden robe, only it was a cheap, vivid yellow nylon sheet bought from Woolworths that generated a power station's worth of static each time they'd moved together. Jim imagined that they'd glowed in the darkness. But the electricity hadn't inhibited them at all.

Jim rubbed his eyes. He deliberately broke the spell. He knew he had to go and speak to Hannah in person and warn her. He had to get out in front of this whole issue and come clean. Honesty was the best policy. Even if was too late. Even if the secret recipe – if that's what the hackers were after – had been compromised already and a competitor was imitating it at that very moment – he had to be the one to make the first move. His company's relationship with SilasFoods depended on it. The jobs of the people he employed depended on it. Perhaps the livelihoods of the people of Silas, Connecticut did too. And, most of all, his relationship with Hannah was in danger. They'd done such a good job keeping a false wall of close friendship between the present and their past that they'd become too cosy, too relaxed.

This was the moment to change. The moment to, perhaps, go back in time so they could build new futures for themselves.

Jim sat back and watched Taryn turn the song into something totally new.

***

WildCat8 (Online)

WildCat8
Satisfied client(s) – great work – quick too –
quite an industry you got going

NicholsonWay
Don't call me Ishmael, call me Henry Ford

WildCat8
R you as arrogant as Ford?

NicholsonWay
Arrogant? Me? Yeah! The best can afford to be.
Any more assignments gratefully received –
spread the word

When Jim called to set up a meeting with Hannah he knew that something was wrong. Her voice was softer, strangely, more intimate.

"Did you know we were whales?" she said.

"Not till yesterday."

"We need to meet – we need to talk…"

"Two whales meeting in an ocean of… doubt," Jim said.

Hannah chuckled, "You were always such a bad phrase-maker."

"Sorry. Nothing changes."

"This is bad, Jim… very bad."

"I know."

"There's no blame… I mean… there's no… suggestion of culpability here… this is… an attack on us. We should have been more prepared, but it's an attack and we are the victims. You understand that don't you?" Hannah said.

"I think so." Jim didn't want to calculate what the loss of the SilasFoods account would cost him – and the people who worked for him – and the town of Peekskill where most of his employees lived. A cold pulse of fear made him catch his breath.

"Let's get together… today… can you get to Olana?"

Jim was about to suggest they do their meeting at the Hudson Valley River Museum – but she seemed determined to go to Olana, the home of Frederic Church. Jim didn't want to go to Olana. It held too many memories.

"Meet me there in two hours." She ended the call.

***

Olana is a gothic pile in Hudson, New York, and Jim had

felt strange searching online it to get the zip code. Back in 1983, when he'd gone there with Brandon Miles and Hannah Cohen (her maiden name) they'd piled duffel bags full of clothes and books into Brandon's growling but sensitive convertible and just headed in the house's general direction. They'd got there without the aid of a GPS or their smartphones. They'd followed their noses and the confusing New York State road signs.

Jim programmed the GPS and sat with his hands on the steering wheel for what seemed like a moment, but was actually five minutes. A knock on the passenger door jolted him out of his reverie. It was Taryn. The morning sun was caught in her hair and she looked, for a moment, like a demure angel.

Jim pressed a button and the glass glided down with an expensive *shhh*.

"You OK?" she asked.

"No."

"Oh…"

"Your band is good. You should get a recording contract," Jim said.

"Yeah, sure, I'll go out and get one now. Down at Staples… or Stop & Shop…."

"Sorry…"

"Was I being too sarcastic?"

"I deserve it. This has, like… hit you hard… the security thing…" Taryn was unsure of herself, as if she'd just realized that she was actually talking to the CEO of the company she worked for – and speaking to him as if she were either his friend or his equal.

"It has. Not just because… it's business… my business…

my professional pride... all that. Not just that. Not just because... I'd taken my eye off the ball, been blasé... all those words, all those clichés. But because it's... opened up something I didn't expect would return. I'd gone all these years assuming that Hannah and I were friends and... we are but..." Jim stopped himself. Taryn knew nothing of his relationship with Hannah back in the 1980s and he didn't want to start pouring his heart out to this... this girl.

"Yeah, I know... it's like when your email gets hacked and everyone in your address book gets some stupid thing about a weight-loss miracle and you realize you still have the email addresses of your ex-boyfriends or bitchy high-school girls who you hated then and still hate now... and they start emailing you back saying 'hey, you still around' or 'hey, your email got hacked and you're still a geeky bitch.' That's bad. That's what I hate about digital stuff. If I could go back to envelopes and stamps, I would."

Jim nodded. He pressed the start button and the car's engine purred into life. He smiled, no keys, no fobs, nothing to hold in your hand and put in your pocket... just a button.

"OK... better be off," Jim said.

Taryn smiled, stood back and waved goodbye as Jim pulled out of the Baines Packaging parking lot – his own, dedicated space; Jim Baines, CEO.

***

Frederic Edwin Church created sumptuous paintings. Landscapes that defined the Hudson River Valley at a time when it was still, mostly, virgin territory and it still looked that way from the brow of the hill where the gothic, Italianate pile sat. Jim could never look at the New England landscape without thinking about the England back home. Back where he was born. It was beautiful but lived in. Here, at the right angle, you could look out and just see rolling, wooded hills and a big, big sky. America. Just like Church's paintings.

Hannah turned to Jim and said, "It's over. I've resigned. I had to. I'm done. I was the obvious candidate to fall on their sword."

"No! Hannah, no!" Jim was stunned.

"It's not your fault." Hannah turned back to the view. "It's what goes with the territory. You get to the top and sometimes you stop thinking like... like an ordinary mortal. You think you're immune. None of us are immune however important we think we are." She sighed deeply and then took a deep breath as if to cleanse her lungs.

"What do we do?" Jim asked after a long minute.

"What are we really afraid of, Jim? You and I? Board members and important people like us? What are we really concerned about?"

"Our businesses..."

"Our pensions. Our reputations. Our inability to keep up with technology. Are those the things we're really worried about?"

Jim turned to look at Hannah. The slightly pink light of a fading afternoon made her look 20 years younger. He caught his breath. Were they still kids? Despite all they'd achieved? Just kids round a board table?

"This is bad. I won't deny it. We'd suspected for a long time that... certain competitors... were after details of what we were planning, but, hey industrial espionage is the third oldest profession isn't it?" She chuckled. She put a hand over her eyes and turned toward the sun.

"What do we do?" Jim said.

"We don't panic. That's the first thing. I need a new career – but that's fine. It might be good for me to start over. You? Well, you're in trouble Jim. I'm sorry, but you are. SilasFoods has brought in the FBI. It will get messy. For both of us. Your current contracts with Silas have been put on hold and there's no chance of future work till... till this thing is resolved." Hannah turned to face Jim. She was being serious, but there was no anger in her eyes.

Jim's head was spinning. Hannah's career was over. His firm might be on the brink of bankruptcy, and all the people who worked for him – half the town! – might be out of a job. Maybe panic was his only option! Jim tried to keep it together. He had to blame someone – find the root cause – the person behind all this, and their motive.

"I have a really bad feeling about... Brandon Miles and his friend request," Jim said.

"Me too. You accepted it. I didn't. He may have nothing to do with this... or everything to do with it. Either way I'd like to know the truth. For my own peace of mind, and yours too, maybe."

Jim nodded. She was right. They needed to know the truth.

Hannah turned to look at the view. It was getting colder. A sudden chill. She shivered. She turned to look at him and gripped his hand tightly. "Where did this disaster spring from and why? It's so unfair... so... random... so... unexpected," she said.

"I wish I knew, and I want to do something about it," Jim said.

Hannah looked at him. Her eyes questioning his statement; challenging him to make it more than just words.

"I want to find whoever did this and confront them, face to face," Jim said. He put his arm around her waist and pulled her closer.

***

WildCat8 (Online)

WildCat8
And lo – another little project

NicholsonWay
Big whales?

WildCat8
Bigger

NicholsonWay
Like it – I'm done with whaling for beginners.

To be continued...

CYBER RESILIENCE IS MORE IMPORTANT THAN EVER BEFORE

In 2013 the Lloyd's Risk Index showed that cyber risk had jumped from 16th on C-level executives' priority list to **third** in just two years. The number of risks has grown exponentially since!

Bluefish Communications

"**90%** of organizations say that maintaining security and privacy in a highly connected world is imperative. **BUT** only 22% believe their current IT and communications facilities enable fully effective management of security and access."

Vodafone Business Ready – 2014

"**55%** of costly cyber-crimes are caused by malicious insiders, denial of services and web-based attacks."

HP & Ponemon Institute LLC, Oct, 2014

"**94%** of businesses have suffered cyber-security incidents"

Kaspersky, Oct, 2014

"**78%** of large organizations were attacked by an unauthorised outsider in the last year"

Arbor Networks Sept, 2014

"Security experts say cyber criminals are increasingly targeting the $3 trillion US healthcare industry, which has many companies still reliant on ageing computer systems that do not use the latest security features."

The Guardian, February 5th 2015

"There has been a massive jump in the number of very large [Denial of Service] attacks... in 2014 we saw more volumetric attacks, with attackers trying to knock people offline by saturating their access to the internet."

Darren Anstee, Arbor Networks, quoted in 'Hacktivists Step up Web Attack Volumes,' BBC News online 27th January 2015

"A business-driven secure architecture can only be developed in parallel with the business strategy. That strategy must emerge from discussions led by the CIO and business leaders and should be translated into a target capability map and systems manifesto."

'Protecting the enterprise with cybersecure IT architecture' by Oliver Bossert, Wolf Richter & Allen Weinberg. McKinsey & Co, March 2015

ABOUT THE AUTHOR

Jerome Vincent has been a script and copy writer for many years and has written widely about corporate technology issues for many of the world's leading multinationals. He's also written copy and films for heritage sites and museums, including Hampton Court Palace, The House of Commons, and The Tower of London, amongst many others. His broadcast work includes 15 plays for BBC Radio 4 and TV documentaries for the BBC and Channel 5. He has written three children's TV series as well as an educational series for BBC Bitesize. He has one feature film under his belt, **Chasing the Deer,** which starred Brian Blessed, and has just finished writing the second series of the comedy show he created, **The Future of Radio**, for BBC Radio 4 (with Stephen Dinsdale).

Misha Glenny is an award winning investigative journalist, author and broadcaster and is the former central Europe correspondent for the Guardian and the BBC. His books include 'McMafia: Seriously Organised Crime' and 'DarkMarket: How Hackers Became the New Mafia' and he is recognised as one of the world's leading experts on cybercrime and global criminal networks. His awards include the Sony Gold Award for outstanding contribution to broadcasting.

He has been regularly consulted by the US and European governments on major policy issues and ran an NGO for three years, assisting with the reconstruction of Serbia, Macedonia and Kosovo.